THE WORLDWALKERS

About the Editor:

Abha Iyengar is an award winning, internationally published writer, editor, translator (Hindi to English), and a British Council - certified creative writing mentor. She is the founder of Creative Wings Studio, where she mentors aspiring authors. She has 8 published books to her credit. Find her at www.abhaiyengar.com

Beta reading:

Taanvii Gupta, Viveka Gupta, Indrani Pillai, Neethu Shashidharan.

Cover illustration:

Trupti Gupta (AI Modified)

Interior illustration:

Trupti Gupta

OrangeBooks Publication

1st Floor, Rajhans Arcade, Mall Road, Kohka, Bhilai, Chhattisgarh 490020
Website: **www.orangebooks.in**

First Edition, 2025

ISBN: 978-93-7426-960-2

Price: Rs. 320.00

Printed in India

THE WORLDWALKERS

Trupti J Gupta

OrangeBooks Publication
www.orangebooks.in

Worldwalkers are the unsung heroes of the Universes,
burning away years of their own lives to lead back lost souls.

For my brave little baby girls,

Pixie and Sia.

CONTENTS

PROLOGUE

The Shadow God was vexed. The souls in his domain were going missing from right under his nose.

This was the work of a demon, he knew it. He needed to set a trap for this slippery devil and rescue all the souls to maintain the balance in the Universe.

✦

Her day started with a massive headache. It was unrelenting, pulsating through her entire being. She pushed herself to get to work, leaving both her girls in the care of the dogsitter.

As the day dragged on, the headache subsided a bit, giving her a false sense of comfort. Even so, at lunch, she was ready to get home, her body completely exhausted.

She rested her head on her work desk. 'Just for a while,' she assured herself, not knowing when she slipped into unconsciousness.

When she opened her eyes, she found herself surrounded by her colleagues fussing over her. Utterly confused, she asked them what was going on, but her voice was lost, and she realized she could not form any words. She heard someone say,

"Hospital!"

She tried to argue, to say, "No hospital!" because she hated hospitals; it had always been a place where one thing led to another, leaving the patient with a huge bill and small relief. She just wanted to get home and cuddle up with her girls. They were her safe space.

But her vomiting had garbled speech, and no one understood a word of what she was saying, including herself.

Everything that followed was a blur of different moments. There were people talking.

"Minipress," someone kept saying. She made a vague connection that something was really not right. She felt the needle stuck in her hand and shook it violently, trying to get it out.

'Don't do that! Idiot!' the still present part of her mind berated her. But she was having none of it! She knew that she had royally pissed someone off because the next moment, somebody grabbed her hand and tied it to the rail of the bed.

The next time she woke up, she realised through her haze that she was being given a bath. She was embarrassed out of her mind, but found herself unable to even cover herself up.

Then, later, someone was roughly yanking on her hair, buzzing it off. She endured the rough handling of her head as the razor dragged across her scalp, utterly unforgiving. Clumps of hair fell to the floor. Though the fact that she was not throwing a huge tantrum over this surprised her. She promised herself she would pummel this person to a pulp when she was able.

She had finally found a haircut that did not make her look like a boiled potato, and here was this moron cutting it all off. She wanted to cry!

The next time she woke, there were machines beeping around her and the scent of the sterile hospital filled her nose.

What was in store for her? She was scared now. Her soul called out to the two little angels she had left back at home.

CHAPTER 1

A Storm on the Horizon

'Lazy days are undoubtedly the best! But even better, are lazy weekends! The fact that Mom is at home on weekends just adds to their charm,' Pixie thought as she snuggled closer to Mom.

✦

Cuddling up with Mom all day, as everyday life moved on outside, was their absolute favourite pastime. Pixie was calm, understanding and would do anything to avoid conflict. Sia, on the other hand, was a short little firecracker of a dog and was always ready to fight Pixie for the most comfortable spot on the bed.

✦

Through all the heat, there was an unshakable feeling that somewhere, far in the distance, a nasty storm was brewing. The girls could practically see it, it's grey clouds shooting out crackling lightning in its quest to appear menacing. It was going to be a formidable storm, they felt numb at the prospect of facing the monstrosity that rolled closer in with every passing second. Even so, they would fight it with all they had.

Much as they tried to keep their spirits up, uncertainty was making a home in their hearts and anxiety was beginning to set in.

✦

They had just finished their evening stroll and got back home, winding down for the night, when they caught the whiff of a familiar scent in the air. This was a scent they knew well, but was not one they were expecting.

"What a great surprise!" Pixie perked up, and Sia's ever-wagging tail wagged even faster, if that was possible.

"Yea!" she said and ran to the door just as the doorbell rang. Their sitter opened the door.

They barked with joy as their guests entered the house. They wiggled between their grandma, grandpa and their aunts, who showered them with love and praises. Through all the welcome chaos, Pixie sensed that something was amiss. She hung back a bit as Sia continued wiggling between all the guests, almost tripping one of the aunts. Something was definitely not right. All their energies were off. It was like they were expecting the worst news possible to walk in through the door right behind them.

Pixie and Sia were still waiting to see their human. 'She is never this late,' they thought. She had promised them that she'd be back soon when she had kissed them goodbye this morning. She had never broken her promise. Not once. So why now?

✦

'The storm is here,' Pixie thought. Between the unexpected arrival of their guests and the suspicious absence of their Mom, they gathered that 'Mom must be in trouble!'

They plopped down and uneasily settled in their spots to rest for the fast-growing night, their aunts patting them to sleep.

The pink blush that had scattered through the sky, turned to a deep shade of blue as time rolled on. Soon, the dead of the night dulled their senses, and their eyes drifted shut. Sounds faded to the back of their minds as they stepped through the night's veil into the land of dreams. Though they were off dreaming, their souls stayed ever alert. Ready to chase away anything that would dare come in and rattle their world.

Both were happily off dreaming when the colours of their dreams shattered and came crashing down around them as a resounding snap echoed through the night.

CHAPTER 2

SNAP

They woke with a start. Eyes flying open. Searching for what might have so utterly shaken their world. It was unmistakable. Something had broken.

"Pix," Sia trembled, curling into herself, "you heard that?" There was a quiver in her voice. Her eyes were as wide as saucers.

"Yes." Pixie was searching for what could have caused the sound. "That was no ordinary sound," she said nervously, as she curiously peered out the window.

Somewhere in the background, their guests were engaged in a serious discussion. Their voices were low and grave. None of them seemed to have heard what the girls had. Everything else remained unmoved. The sound was *meant* to be heard only by the two of them. This was a piece of vital information; it told them that the resounding snap was not of anything physical. Pixie looked, squinting her eyes. Her heart beating hard in her chest, she carefully scanned the space outside the window, looking for anything that would count as out of the ordinary. Sia sat beside her and joined in her search.

Far in the distance, a thin silvery string fluttered in the silent breeze of the night.

"Pix, look!" Sia said as she stayed zeroed in on the gently undulating string shimmering in the night sky, afraid to lose sight of it.

Pixie followed Sia's gaze and quickly spotted the innocently swaying string. It was easy to miss. A little way above it was a dot of glowing light pulsating with the rhythm of a heartbeat. That was not a star. She knew exactly what that was!

Pixie instantly put two and two together.

"Oh, no!" she gasped. "Sia, this is not good! Something has happened to Mom. Her soul has detached from Earth. We must do something before it is lost to the

Universe forever!" The panic in Pixie's voice was pronounced. "Si, we have to go get her!"

"Umm. How?" Sia looked at her sister, confused. What could they possibly do?

"We are Worldwalkers, Si. If anyone *can* do something, it's us."

"We can lead lost souls back. We are the guardians of Mom's soul and have a strong bond with it. The fact that there was such a loud snap, means that the Earth plane was holding on to the soul. The soul might have unfinished business. Also, we heard the sound, is the Earth's way of telling us that we need to follow her soul and guide it back."

A fire lit in Sia's eyes. If by doing this, it meant that they would be able to see Mom again, then she would put her life on the line. No question!

"Si. Are you ready?" Pixie asked, her eyes still

tracking the tiny speck in the sky. Not getting any reply, she looked back. Her heart softened at the sight of Sia's little body, trembling with fear. She smiled when she looked at her sister's eyes, though. Despite her apprehension, Sia's eyes held the ferocity of a lioness ready to fight anything to bring her person back.

"Si, we'll stay close to each other and will be back with Mom in a flash!" Pixie reassured her, understanding that this was new for Sia. "We'll be fine. Don't worry, there are always other Worldwalkers travelling around and willing to lend a hand. We won't be alone. You'll see."

Sia gave a curt nod. "You should stay behind me Pix," she said, her eyes burning with determination, even as another wave of fear coursed through her. "The Universe is a scary place. I can protect you! We should hurry! Her soul is getting away, Pix!" Sia's eyes traced the tiny dot floating further away in the night-sky.

Pixie nodded, “Remember, Si, once we step into the ‘spirit plane,’ we will quickly have to make a deal with one of the World walkers waiting around us.”

Then, finding her own spark of courage, she casually stepped out of her physical form and Sia followed suit.

With no soul to hold their physical forms upright, their bodies collapsed to the floor. Worldwalkers could not just leave their physical forms unoccupied, so they had the freedom to lend them to other Worldwalkers as temporary refuge until they returned. But obviously, they had to judge, who their soul’s frequency matched with best, to make a deal.

Deals between Worldwalkers were eternally binding contracts that, if broken, had the power to bring down divine judgment on the soul that was in the wrong.

Pixie had learnt the hard way that a deal needed to be negotiated. When once, she had returned after a quick stroll around the moon, only to find that a pompous cat's soul had taken up residence in her body. Though she had nothing personal against cats, it was shocking to say the least! And aggravating even more when the cat refused to leave, strutting around like it owned the place. "I have done you a huge favour," the cat had told her. "You should be grateful that I saved your body from rotting away!"

Now, because there had been no contract between Pixie and the cat, Pixie had had to wait patiently and watch as the cat treated her, then human - like trash and pick fights with practically everyone. It had taken Pixie forever to coax the cat into returning her body. 'Never again!' she had thought. It had been a while before she had stepped into the 'spirit plane' again, after the incident.

Eventually, she had learnt how to make deals from one of her many friends, who had blatantly laughed in her face for her stupidity.

Once Pixie and Sia had negotiated their own deals, positive that no one would notice their absence, they bounded out the window into the crisp night, ready to begin their chase as Worldwalkers.

✦

Worldwalkers are souls who can travel in and out of different realms and move through dimensions with ease, if they know what to look for and how to navigate the pitch-black of the Universe. Sia was still new to this whole Worldwalking business, but Pixie was a pro and was very good at it. She had travelled through different realms more times than she could count. On many occasions, to help a friend and at other times to simply travel, observe and learn.

Pixie had guided Sia through how to navigate the Universe. But those were just some basic lessons. What they were about to attempt now was far more dangerous than just a stroll through their neighbourhood planets.

Universes, by nature were unforgiving and lived by the motto of 'an eye for an eye.' They were about to trade years of their own lives to get their Mom's soul back. Ever wonder why the lives of so many animals are so short?

✦

Worldwalkers are the unsung superheroes of the Universes. They burn years of their own lives like fuel when they choose to lead any lost souls to safety and they do so without expecting anything in return.

✦

And so, Pixie and Sia ran, free from the confines of their physical bodies. They leapt through the cool night air with their sights firmly set on the tiny glowing speck floating in the distance.

This would be easy if they could catch the soul before it crossed over to some other dimension, as every soul inevitably did. They were close now, so close! A loud bang from somewhere below shattered the fragile silence, startling them. They looked down to see a spray of sparkly lights bloom and fill the sky before it crackled and faded away. The sound must have spooked Mom's soul because in an instant, it flickered and vanished.

Honestly, humans and their firecrackers! Pixie was absolutely tired of it. Through her many, many lifetimes, she failed to understand humanity's obsession with creating so much unnecessary noise. 'It's a mystery that will probably remain unsolved forever,' she thought.

Pixie looked back at Sia, who was trembling. Sia didn't do so well with new things and loud noises and this situation was both of those things, packaged into one pretty little box of chaos.

Honestly speaking, neither did Pixie, but she was far older than Sia was and was fairly used to human shenanigans.

Sia, noticing that Pixie was a bit too far away, suddenly scrambled to catch up with her. "Pix," she said, "do you feel that weird feeling in your stomach?"

"Yes," Pixie acknowledged her sister's question as she felt the unmistakable tug.

"What is that?" Sia asked, her head tilting.

"It's the cord that bonds our souls to Mom's soul."

"Does everyone have this cord?"

"Souls that are closely bonded have the cord connection."

"Then why aren't Grandma and Grandpa, and aunties here with us, chasing after Mom?"

"Not everyone can break free of their physical bodies like we can, Si," Pixie explained. "They feel the tug, yes, but they are powerless. What we're feeling will manifest for them as helplessness, sadness, and anxiety.

It's the worst situation to be in."

She continued, "They can't follow the soul. Not that they don't want to. But they're just not equipped for that, like we are. So, let's go save her, for us all!"

"Yeah!" Sia hopped around, her fear gone, her ears flopping about and her tail wagging, "let's!"

The cord connecting them to Mom would be their guide to wherever the soul went. They felt a tug that pulled them into a starkly different place. Both stood there, floating high above some unknown world with raging purple clouds swirling around them. Sia moved closer to Pixie. It was all utterly disorienting. Through the rolling mist and chaos, they spotted the white speck of the soul, darting downward, ready to explore this new place. They dashed towards it. Only for it to flicker and vanish again.

CHAPTER 3

FLIGHT

The soul was keen to explore. Speeding ahead as though it had tasted freedom for the first time. They were locked in a never-ending game of chase-your-tail, getting dragged from one world to another, like rapidly flicking through all the many channels the Universe had to offer. It was getting difficult to keep track of how many worlds they had crossed. Bounding over giant flowers. Narrowly missing the razor-sharp snap of some unknown creature. Swimming through the depths of some toxic-looking ocean with snake-like creatures swarming them. Just as one of the creatures lunged for them, they were suddenly floating through a dense space cloud.

One time, they had materialised in the middle of what looked like a serious meeting of sorts. It was a huge room that held row after row of several creatures keenly listening to the discussion in progress.

"If the beings of Gaia do not show restraint, we are afraid we will have to intervene," one of them said. The statement gained approving nods from many others, causing a stir of murmur in the otherwise quiet room. The soul stayed put here; it seemed interested in the conversation that was unfolding.

Pixie nudged Sia, and they took the chance to sneak closer to the soul. Suddenly, everything went silent. All the creatures in the room were staring right at them. The soul flickered and vanished, as though it had been caught doing something off-limits, pulling Pixie and Sia along.

When they materialised again, the soul was once more far away from them. Though they were chasing it at top speed, the distance between them and the soul did not seem to reduce.

"Lost?" They heard a voice. Coming to a sharp stop, they turned to look at who it was.

"Fluffers?" Pixie asked, her voice cautious. She instinctively stepped in front of Sia, whose hackles were already up, ready to snap at this new guest.

"Si, wait!" Pixie tried to calm her down. "We know him. It's Fluffers."

"I know," Sia fumed, "I don't like him."

Fluffers was an abandoned German Shepherd they had met on one of their walks. Sia had an eternal grudge against German Shepherds, Huskies and Labradors, basically, any dog that was bigger than she was. Pixie was the sole exception, for which Pixie had always thanked her lucky stars.

Unlike Pixie, who had instantly struck up a friendship with Fluffers, Sia had wanted to shred the old dog to ribbons every time she saw him.

Pixie had found that walks were never a dull affair, thanks to Sia's little quirk. It was very entertaining to watch any handler wrestle Sia back and away from dogs, who she clearly wanted to reduce to a rubble. She paid little mind to the fact that the dogs she wanted to attack could easily overpower her in a heartbeat. It was cute, Pixie had thought, the way Sia was so sure that she could take them on all by herself. Pixie would merely stand back and watch this tiny thing snap at empty air in front of her, and sometimes also at the handler's hand if it got in the way of her and her oversize target.

The first time they had met Fluffers, he had been completely taken aback by Sia's unwarranted reaction at the mere sight of him. But he had quickly shrugged it off, understanding that Sia was a young soul and would soon learn that not everyone was out to hurt her.

"Lost?" he repeated, paying little mind to Sia's visceral reaction.

"The soul in our care left the Earth plane suddenly. We are chasing after it to bring it back," Pixie said, still standing between Fluffers and Sia.

"Maybe you should let the soul go. There are some things that we can't control, you know this, Pix."

Sia suddenly shot past Pixie and tackled Fluffers down. They tumbled through the dark of outer space, coming to a stop with Sia atop Fluffers, teeth bared and snapping her jaws at the old dog.

"Don't patronize her," she snarled. "It's not our soul's time!"

"Ok, ok," Fluffers said, his ears pressed down to his head, "I get you."

"Do you?" Sia growled.

Pixie placed a paw on Sia's back. "Si," she calmly said, "we have to go." They were feeling the soul's tug on them. It had already vanished again.

There it was, the tug. And again. And again, and then, without warning, it was gone.

What? Pixie felt utterly abandoned. She concentrated all her senses inward, trying to find any trace of the tug, but it was of no use.

She was a panicked mess. Tears welled up in her eyes. “It’s gone,” she sniffled, her heart shattering into a million pieces. She looked around like a lost puppy for any sign of the soul.

“I can’t feel the pull anymore,” her voice was thick as her throat closed up with building tears.

“I can’t feel it either,” Sia said, her eyes darting around, tears falling freely.

They stood there, in the unforgiving cold and dark of the Universe with no hint of what direction to go in next. Pixie sat close to Sia, trying to comfort her.

“Hey now,” Fluffers spoke softly. “Nothing’s lost,” he said, looking at their crestfallen faces.

Sia shot him an angry glare, making the old dog cower. "This is all your fault! By the way, grandpa!" she snapped at him. "Thanks for distracting us!"

"Partly," he said, "yes, I agree."

He walked over and sat next to Pixie. "Just hear me out, ok," he said, "There is still a chance you can find the soul."

"There is? How?" Pixie's voice was wobbly. Her sad eyes met Fluffers' calm ones.

"If you can't feel the tug, chances are the soul will have ventured into the dark dimension of the Universe."

Pixie gasped, "That place is a maze!" Her voice trembled as memories of the place flooded her mind. "I was hoping to catch Mom's soul without having to go in there at all."

"So, you've been there?"

"Yes, once. Though I don't really remember entering the place," Pixie shivered, "or how I got out."

"Look, I've been there far too many times," Fluffers said, with a wise man's confidence. "If you stick with me, I can be your guide."

Sia was listening intently, her eyes darting from one to the other.

"What is this place?" she finally managed. Curiosity playing in her eyes.

"The Dark," Fluffers took a weary breath, "dimension is where souls can slip off to. The Universe is cruel. But sometimes it just must be. There are a finite number of souls, you see, and the Universe needs to recycle and reuse. So, it has created a dimension where it traps souls and keeps them there till they forget everything about their past lives. Once the souls are deemed ready, they are transferred to other planets and places that need them. Some souls like us Worldwalkers, get to choose the planet we go to. We are allowed to keep most of our memories. Our souls are made of hardy stuff. But, that is not true for all souls. So, the Universe must erase the memories of these souls to make sure that they don't crumble under the pressure of excessive memories, only to wither away and become useless stardust."

"Wow, I am way too young." Sia looked at Fluffers with newfound amazement, taking in every word he said. "And you are way too old," she added unnecessarily.

"Yes," Fluffers chuckled, placing a gentle paw on Sia's head, who instantly wiggled out from under it, "I am."

"And," Sia said, her tone sceptical, "how many times have you been to this 'dark dimension' that we can trust you to be our guide?"

"Many enough."

"I'll haunt you if we get lost or die in there!" Sia growled.

"That's a truly scary thought, Sia!" Fluffers feigned fear and let a fake shudder rattle through him.

CHAPTER 4

Into the Dark Dimension

"The Universe can be scary but if you have the right mindset and know what to look for," Fluffers said, "it's a pretty great place, like an amusement park!"

They followed as Fluffers led the way, reaching some godforsaken corner of this Universe. This place was pitch black. It had no planets, no stars, not even that one rogue asteroid shooting by. Here, literally in the middle of nowhere, it was completely disorienting. They had put all their trust in Fluffers to guide them into the Dark dimension. Apparently, one could only enter the place from a rift in the middle of nowhere, at the point where two Universes met. So, that was where the three of them were headed.

"You sure this is the way, Fluffers?" Pixie asked, as she looked around.

"Of course! Matter of fact, we're almost there," Fluffers casually stated.

The darkness around them was pressing in on them; as though it was deliberately conspiring to confuse them.

Pixie and Sia were both amazed at the confidence with which Fluffers navigated the place completely undaunted.

'No wonder so many souls get lost.' Pixie thought.

As though treading Pixie's mind, "Someone should put up some direction signs," Sia pointed out. "How do you know where to go? I mean, Fluffers, you must have been really jobless to actually figure out how to find this place."

"Hey!" Fluffers was not happy with that comment. "You should thank your lucky stars I was 'jobless'. We can stop if you want to keep running your smart mouth!"

“I thought you were here because you wanted to fix a mistake *you* made,” Sia shot back at him. “We wouldn’t have to thank any stars if you hadn’t butt in.”

“She is sorry.” Pixie tried to break the tension. “Aren’t you, Si?”

“No,” was the low mumble of a reply she got.

“She is,” Pixie grinned at Fluffers, who continued moving ahead, and they resumed their journey.

They had gone a little way ahead when Fluffers came to a sudden stop. “Look, did you see that?”

“See what?” Sia stared intently, narrowing her eyes, trying to see what Fluffers was referring to. “I think your eyes are dying, you old dog. You’re seeing things. There is nothing there.”

“Just follow close.”

They moved closer to Fluffers, squinting their eyes, trying to figure out what the older dog was claiming to see.

"Ooh, I see it!" Sia practically jumped with excitement. Then Pixie saw it too.

It looked like a large shard of glass.

"What *is* that?" The amazement in Sia's voice was apparent.

"It's one of the entrances into the dark dimension. Come on!" Fluffers shot ahead towards the doorway, stopping every few paces for Pixie and Sia to catch up.

They reached the very edge of the doorway.

"Come on," Fluffers said. Pixie and Sia braced themselves, fully expecting to bump into the glass-like surface, but they didn't, and they passed right through it.

They found themselves in a bizarre space. A room, of sorts, with big and small jagged shards of glass sticking out at various angles, some stretching from the floor to the ceiling. It was almost pitch dark, save for the occasional flash of an image or reflection in one of the many glass-like surfaces. “Be careful,” Fluffers cautioned when they got too close to the edge of one of the shards, “this stuff can cut through souls.”

“I rarely get visitors here,” a deep voice startled them, freezing them in their tracks. “But I’m not surprised it's you, Young man!” Fluffers looked like he wanted to bolt out of there.

They felt an unseen force pulling them. It was utterly freaky and sent chills coursing through the three of them.

They came to a sudden stop in front of a fragmented wall, their own reflections staring back at them. The wall moved, a ripple running over it. and something resembling a face formed in its fragmented surface. Was it a face? It shifted before any of them could make any sense of what they were looking at here. Then it shifted again. It looked like a lizard? When it shifted again and formed something they entirely did not recognize. It kept shifting and morphing into many different types of faces, making a tinkling sound as it changed.

Finally, it spoke.

"What are three Worldwalkers doing in my domain?" it said in a voice that also felt fragmented in its own way, like crackling glass.

"What *is* that thing?" Pixie asked Fluffers, her voice turned into a low, terrified whisper.

Fluffers whispered back, "That's the Shadow god, the one with a million faces. He guards the entrances into the dark dimension."

"A *GOD*?!" Sia whispered to Pixie, who looked equally impressed and terrified.

"Could have warned us in advance, Fluffers," Sia berated the older dog, "that we'll be meeting a creepy god."

The Shadow god spoke directly to Fluffers. "I'm glad to see you again, Fluffers! But you need to stop strolling in here with your friends."

Pixie and Sia watched as this weird thing addressed the old dog, who was currently cowering with his tail tucked in between his legs.

"Glad to see you too! Sir, Shadow god, sir!" Fluffers said, with a nervous laugh.

"I told you to stay out of this place, Fluffers. Listen. Before something bad ends up happening." The Shadow god reprimanded Fluffers, his voice booming, its glassy quality sharpened.

"Umm, y-yes, sir. But you see, my friends here needed some help."

"Isn't that always your excuse, Fluffers?" The Shadow god turned to look at Pixie and Sia, who involuntarily shrank under his gaze.

"Actually," the god said, "*nobody* needs to have any business in my domain."

The Shadow god gave Pixie and Sia a sceptical look. "So, what *is* your problem?"

Pixie and Sia just stared mutely at the bizarre, fragmented, glassy thing that was waiting for their reply.

"The soul they were supposed to protect…" Fluffers started.

"Tch," the Shadow god tutted at Fluffers, silencing him instantly. "I'm talking to these two, young man."

"Y-yes, sir," Fluffers averted his gaze, pulling on his best rendition of the guilty face.

Pixie cleared her throat, breaking the silence, "You see, sir god, a soul we were charged with guarding was unexpectedly ripped from our realm and has maybe managed to find its way in here."

"Little one," the Shadow god got in close to Pixie's face and her eyes widened in absolute fear, "if a soul has managed to find its way in here, it's *almost* never by accident. So, I'd suggest you let it be and leave. Working on a 'maybe' is not something I would advise you to do here. This place is dangerous."

"We are counting on the *'almost'* part of this situation, s-sir," Pixie managed to sputter. She was pretty sure that if she had been in her physical body, she'd have peed herself and made a bit of a mess. But she had surprised herself as she stood her ground and spoke with this abnormal and creepy god.

"I like your wit, little one," the Shadow god said as the face retracted back into the fragmented wall, leaving a surface of sparkly, undulating shards in front of them.

Moments later, a humanoid figure emerged from that same wall. This figure was of a more reasonable size, the 'normal' that the three of them were accustomed to. Even though the size was a welcome change, it was still made of the same strange glass-shard-like material that tinkled and clinked every time the god moved.

Clink. Clink. Clink.

"Who is this soul you're so concerned about?" the Shadow god asked as he walked over to them.

"The soul is our person. We are its guardians!" Sia piped in.

"Oh," the god shifted his attention to Sia, "I thought you had no words, little one. I'm glad you can speak."

"Of course I have 'words,'' Sia looked offended. "If you are a god," she added, "you should know who has what!"

"I am a god, yes," it said, "but I am a god of only this domain." The Shadow god gestured around. "And little one, the notion that gods know everything is entirely preposterous. I'm not God-Source, you know. The God of gods and I doubt even God-Source knows everything considering the giant mess everything has now become."

"There is a god of gods?" Sia was astonished. Her eyes lit up. "Awesome!"

"There is, little one. The god of gods, the god of us all, is God-Source. It's who we all must answer to in the end," the Shadow god said.

✦

"Getting back to the question of your soul, there are many souls that enter this domain at every moment.

They are all lost Souls that have served their purpose in the life they were granted." The Shadow god sighed, as if he was feeling bad for the fate of all the souls. "You say that both of you are the guardians of this soul? If you feel the soul was taken unfairly, you may take back the soul you are here for. But if the soul has finished serving its purpose, it will wither away and will not bond to its physical form. And mind you," the Shadow god's tone became stern, "you may only take the one soul. You do not have permission to take any other. Not even by mistake! Also, for the soul to be able to leave the domain, it will have to remember who you are."

"Ok, that was easy." Sia said, tilting her head at the Shadow god, "You look creepy and scary, but you are nice, actually." This made Pixie and Fluffers dart angry glances at her.

"Are you trying to get us killed or banned?" Fluffers whispered angrily.

The Shadow god let out a clinking laugh. "It's alright, Fluffers. This little one has spirit!" the god said, his ever-shifting smile getting wider. He placed a quick pat on Sia's head that left an undulating, glassy shard there for a moment. Sia shook her head, her ears flapping, trying to shake off the odd sensation on her head.

Fluffers just stared on. He always saw the god as a scary entity. Something about Sia had triggered a lighter side in the otherwise stern and unyielding god.

"Be assured that I'll be watching the three of you. We cannot have sightseers hanging around in here. I am not one of those all-noble gods, but I will have to come to your aid if anything were to happen to any of you, so please do me a favour, get your soul and get out, as soon as possible. I have better things to do," he said. Then turned to Fluffers, "What's Rule one, Fluffers? He asked, catching the old dog off guard.

"Ah." Fluffers thought, "No sneaking out souls?"

"What makes you think we will sneak other souls out of here?" Sia said. "We have better things to do too," she continued. Pixie looked mortified, "Sir," Sia reluctantly added, cowering when the Shadow god shot her an annoyed look.

"Ha!" the Shadow god let out a laugh, "What a spirited little soul you are!" He patted Sia's head again, making her shrink some more into herself.

The god tilted his head in Sia's direction. "Souls that enter this domain are constantly looking for a way out, and they may attach to you. So, you could end up unintentionally bringing them along with you and thus end up sneaking them out."

"We will keep a watch that no such thing happens," Pixie assured the god.

"Then you can be off."

"Thank you, sir god." Fluffers smiled obsequiously at the god.

"And remember, if the soul you are after does not remember you, it will not be allowed to exit. So, pray to all the gods you know."

With that, the Shadow god disappeared and a small portal opened behind them.

CHAPTER 5

BACK TO THE CHASE

They exited the bizarre glassy room and walked right into a pink mist that engulfed them.

"It's a cloud of memories!" Fluffers said. "We need to get out! Fast! If we get trapped here, it will be an endless nightmare. This place is full of souls. The Shadow god did this on purpose. He is testing us. Run! Stay vigilant."

They stayed together as they dashed blindly through the thick, pink cloud, not really seeing where they were going. They soon managed to shoot out of the mist, leaving a sparkly trail behind them. Coming to a stop, they looked at each other and realized that they were all covered in a golden, sparkling glitter-like matter.

Sia's eyes lit up, "So pretty! You look stunning! Pix!" she panted.

Pixie smiled but knew that once they were back home, she would have to keep Sia away from all kinds of glitter. To make matters worse, Mom had a whole lot of that stuff, so she would need to be extra watchful.

"Hey! Look," Fluffers said, the warning in his tone catching their attention. They turned and saw little white creatures filing out of the cloud, following the trail that they had left behind, wisps of which still lingered, connecting them to the huge pink cloud.

Looking at the cute, little, chubby creatures walking towards them, Sia squealed with excitement.

"What *are* those?" she asked.

Each creature had a soft glow around it and had a thin, shiny string dangling out of its belly.

"Souls!" Pixie and Fluffers gasped together.

"They are so cute!" Sia squealed, bouncing in place with stars in her eyes. "Is Mom going to look like this, too, now?"

"No, Si!" Pixie explained, horrified at the thought. "Souls take this appearance only when they are completely stripped of their memories."

Fluffers raised the alarm. "Watch out!" he yelped, pointing behind them. Pixie and Sia turned to see many of the strings attached to the little creatures snaking towards them.

"We need to get this dust off ourselves," Fluffers said urgently, even as he gave himself a thorough shake, sparkly dust flying everywhere and vanishing.

Pixie and Sia followed his lead and the three ducked out of there at once. Running far, far away, in their quest to put distance between themselves and the little soul creatures. As they ran out of reach, the souls that had been following them burst into dust and merged back with the cloud of memories, submitting to their fates once again.

"That was close!" Pixie said to Sia, who looked sad at the sight of the souls returning to the cloud.

"We shouldn't have run," Sia said. "They were harmless!"

"Those souls were trying to attach to us. Remember what the Shadow god said?" Fluffers asked, trying to get Sia to remember the rule.

"That we can't take any other soul outside?" Sia pouted.

"Yes, if a soul attaches to us and creates a bond, it will be difficult to get rid of it."

"Hey! That's a soul you are talking about," Sia got all defensive. "Don't say *'get rid of it'* so casually. We must respect every life, is what Mom always says."

"Yes, you're right, Si," Fluffers said, "We must have respect for every life. I'm sorry."

"It's Sia!" Sia corrected him. Not everyone got to call her 'Si'— that privilege had to be earned.

Pixie rolled her eyes, but Fluffers smiled at Sia's little tantrum; he found it endearing.

✦

Now that they had had a breather, it was time to get back to the business at hand.

"What now, Fluffers?" Pixie asked, as she watched Sia, who was swatting away around herself, lest another soul tries to attach itself to her. This dimension was full of souls of all kinds. Most of them were held in one of the many clouds of memories, but there were some that drifted around aimlessly. It looked like every soul in here was looking for a chance to get out.

'And why wouldn't they?' Sia thought to herself. Who would like all their memories stripped away? The whole ordeal must be so painful. After living a life and creating memories Many of which she cherished more than her very life. She'd rather burst into stardust than have her memories wiped clean.

A few paces away, Pixie watched as Fluffers contemplated their next move while he flicked away the last of that glittery dust that still clung to his furry tail, occasionally glancing at Sia, who was lost in her own thoughts.

"Ok," Fluffers said finally, "let's do this"

"Si!" Pixie called out to her. "Come here."

"But the souls?"

"We will be alert. Don't worry about them."

"Okay," she said as she ran to Pixie and Fluffers.

"Now listen closely," Fluffers said solemnly.

Pixie and Sia shuffled in close, listening intently.

"You need to find and strengthen your connection

with your Mom's soul before the connection vanishes completely. Feel within you and check if you can still sense the soul's pull. However slight."

Both did as they were told, their eyes scrunched shut in concentration.

Pixie opened her eyes, tears brimming on their edges. "It's there," she said. "It's there, but it's so faint."

Sia was still focusing on finding her own connection.

"I can feel it too," she said, as little tears escaped from her eyes. "But Pix is right, it's super faint," she said, opening her eyes. More tears rolled down her face.

"Ok, this is good. Both of you still have the cord connection," he said, his voice thick as he fought back tears of his own. "Here's what both of you will do. Close your eyes, and think of the one you are searching for. Think of the very first day, each of you met the soul. We will be reforging the cord connection from our end."

"It will help the soul remember who it is. And in turn, it will help the soul remember who you both are and the bond that you share."

"How will we know if it's working or not?" Sia asked.

"That's what I'm here for. The soul will be pulled closer towards us, and we will be able to see it as before. I'll let you know when I can see it."

CHAPTER 6

Meeting Pixie A.K.A. Pix

The first thing she remembered was the warmth of her mother's embrace. There were other bodies squirming around her.

She opened her tiny eyes just a crack after what felt like a long, long slumber. This was a fresh new world for her, though very familiar. Looking around, she saw many little creatures just like her, cooing and squirming around. All of them radiated a soft warmth that kept her cosy. Through pure instinct, she looked for her mother. She just knew that she needed to suckle at the nipple to fill up her growling little tummy. Still too young to walk, she wiggled her way over to one and latched on. The warm milk soothed her growing hunger.

Once full, she let go and drifted off to sleep. Through her sleepy haze, she caught sight of her mother, looking down at her, pure love brimming in her eyes. She snuggled in closer.

Days passed, and soon she had grown strong enough to run around with her siblings. They were all familiar with one another now and shared the special kind of bond that only siblings have. Later, she would learn that this was a family bond, a bond that creatures are born with. If one was hurt, the others instinctively knew, no matter how far they were from each other. They might not physically be able to help each other, but they were always with one another in spirit.

Imagine her joy when, a lot later in life, she found out that they were all Worldwalkers. This meant they could have fun together whenever they wanted. It was the best thing ever!

They had started as a litter of eight puppies, making trouble for their mother whenever they could and playing at the bottom of this large structure called a 'building' as the guardian dogs had called it. She, along with her siblings, played all day under the sun. The older dogs in the area kept an eye on them when their mother was away. There were some other creatures around, too. Who were a lot taller and walked on two legs. Taller even than their mother and the guardian dogs. These tall creatures were "humans," their mother had told them.

Some of these humans were kind, and some of them were extremely mean. All the puppies knew that they needed to stay away from the mean humans and run towards the kind ones who picked them up, cuddled them, and played with them. The kind ones fed them whenever they could. They let them into their homes when Mother Nature got angry and soaked everything outside with water that fell from the sky.

She, very early on, understood that the world she had been born in was a harsh place. Her pack of eight puppies had reduced to a meagre five when one by one, her siblings were crushed under these moving things called 'vehicles.' Some of the humans rushed them to a 'doctor,' but in the end, it was of no use; they had passed away. She felt her heart twist in a kind of pain she never wanted to feel again. Ever. She had watched as the humans had buried her siblings' lifeless bodies. She always made it a point to play inside the confines of the building, as her mother said. She even ushered her other siblings inside if they strayed too far out.

She and her brothers and sisters had invented many games. One was the jumping game, where they climbed up some stairs and then jumped down. The winner was the one who could jump from four steps high, which was the current record. They were all growing pups who, at all times, wanted to prove their mettle. So, she climbed onto the fourth step and, in her greed to prove her strength, climbed onto the fifth step, her adventurous feat gaining immediate admiration from her siblings. She felt a swell of pride that crumbled the moment she jumped and landed on the ground, all wrong. Marvelling at her own stupidity when a sharp pain shot up her leg, and a horrible cry left her mouth. Just like the cries she had heard from her siblings who died on the road, under the wheels of those unforgiving vehicle things.

Her pained cry echoed through the entire building and beyond. The agony that ran up and down her injured leg was intense. Still, she limped toward the little burrow her mom had built for them. It was the only place where, in his opinion was truly safe.

Suddenly, the pain in her leg was drastically reduced when someone scooped her up. Through squinted eyes, she tried to see who it was. It was a human. In its arms, she felt comfortable. She wished it would last forever! Little did she know how powerful this wish she had just made was.

The human put her down on flat ground and stroked her injured leg, as if it was trying to take the pain away.

"Oh, poor baby," the human cooed.

"You jumped, didn't you?" the human said in a stern tone, as it wagged its finger at her.

"Silly little girl! You must be careful," the human reprimanded.

She cowered at the tone of the human's voice, understanding her mistake. She was not afraid of the angry human; she was just amazed at her own foolishness!

'Will I die like the others now? Even though I did not step outside the building's safety. Her mind started spinning up the worst scenarios.

The kind human placed her on flat ground, stepped a few paces away and sat down, holding it's palms open.

"Ok, baby girl, come on. Walk to me," it said, "come on, you can do it!" It encouraged her when she hesitated.

She understood what was being asked of her. The human was calling her towards itself. She started walking and caught a glimpse of her mother peeking at her from the doorway that led to the stairs. Putting on her brave face, she tried her best not to limp. She did not want to worry her mother or this human coaxing her to walk, though she knew that her mother would eventually find out. Nothing ever went past her unnoticed.

She took a couple of steps, looked at her mother, then up at the human. Her effort seemed to have satisfied the human.

"That's good! Good girl!" the human said.

It walked up to her again and stroked her leg.

"Does it hurt?" it asked.

'Yes,' she wanted to say. She wanted to cry, it hurt so much! But she did not have the heart to make her mother worry.

Her mother, who had already lost so many of her children. She had watched as her mother had silently cried in their little burrow while everything around them just moved on as if nothing had happened. She had watched helplessly as her mother's heart broke into a million pieces. She wished she could bring them all back so that she could piece her mother's heart back together. But she could not do so. 'It's the rule of the Universe,' she just knew, somehow, she knew. Things that are truly lost are never found again. She knew that the Universe was cruel like that.

The next few days, after her stupid stunt, were a blur. She was slowly getting weaker because she couldn't get to any of the food in time. Thanks to her throbbing leg. Even taking a single step was pure torture. All she could do was watch as the others quickly gobbled up all the food. She swallowed her hunger and put on a smile when her tummy grumbled.

One morning, she sat on a tiny mound of mud and watched her siblings play. She so desperately wanted to join in the fun. But her leg wouldn't allow it.

The human who had helped her when she fell walked into the building. She watched the human intently, and their eyes met. The human immediately knew that something was wrong and strode straight up to her.

'Help me,' her heart reached out to the human. And she was scooped up in the human's arms once again.

"Oh, poor baby girl," the human cooed at her again. "It hurts, right? Let's go to the doctor."

'Doctor!' Alarm bells went off in her head at the sound of the word. That was the word they had said every time one of her siblings had died. The word scared her. *Was she going to die?* She wanted to wiggle out of the secure hold of the human and run. A shiver ran through her body.

The human bundled her up in a warm cloth and gently cradled her as they got into one of those terrifying vehicle things that had crushed her siblings.

She felt sick! But she was too weak to put up a fight. The vehicle they were in moved really fast. The world outside became a blur; everything moved past them way too fast. Wind brushed over her face in waves.

Then, they suddenly stopped, and she was carried out of the vehicle. The human called 'Doctor' looked at her leg. It felt around for a bit, and she could not contain a pained whine.

"It's broken in two places," the doctor said. "We will have to put it in a cast."

She had no idea what all of that meant, but the human who had got her there said, "Yes, let's do that," so confidently that it washed away all her doubts.

And just like that, there was a hard casing all around her leg. It felt awkward but also oddly comforting. The cast meant that she could not bend her leg at all. That was a blessing even if it cost her a bit of discomfort because the pain was substantially low.

She understood then that 'doctor' did not mean that creatures always died; it meant that creatures got help in their worst times. She was alive, after all!

When they got back, all her siblings gathered around her, admiring her new leg ornament, which she flaunted with pride and soaked up all the attention.

The relief from the cast was immense. She could run around to an extent and play a little, too, without pain shooting through her entire body. It was amazing!

When the day ended, the human scooped her up again and stuffed her in a large bag. To say that she was confused would be an understatement. Why was she suddenly in this bag? She wriggled, trying her very best to get out.

"We can't leave you here, baby girl. We need to care for that broken leg," the human said as it held her in place. She watched as all her siblings and her mother looked on. She so desperately wanted to stay there with them.

The human took her to its home. She cautiously got out of the bag and set foot on the glossy floors, as the human watched her. She immediately got to exploring the new place. Really wishing that her siblings were with her because going on adventures was their favourite thing to do.

But as the days passed, nothing of the sort happened.

She did get to see her siblings and Mother every day when the human went to work. But the human brought her back to its home every evening. Soon, the human stopped going there altogether. She was sad at first when she realised that she would not see her siblings and mother. Soon got used to her new life. The human played with her, fed her and cuddled her. Days spent with the human were like a warm dream. She had formed a beautiful bond with the human.

A few days later, they went to the 'doctor' again, and the cast on her leg was taken off. Like magic. The pain was completely gone, and she could move about freely.

She had grown a bit since the human had bought her home. The human had also bought her some toys that she loved playing with.

Abruptly, the human started acting aloof. As if it wanted her to stay away. It broke her heart that the human would not play with her. It felt like the human wanted her to go away. But she had been with the human for quite some time now and knew that, in its heart, the human did not want to stay away. She could tell by the way the human would still pet her.

She could not figure out what the problem was.

"I know you'll be ok, wherever you go," the human told her. She watched as tears brimmed in its eyes and understood then what was happening. The human was pulling away from her; the human wanted to give her away.

It made her sad, and she wondered if she had done something wrong. She could have sworn that she had been on her best behaviour, except for a couple of mishaps when she had pooped on the carpet and peed in the bedroom. And there was that one time when she had tried to growl at the human, making the human pretty mad. So much so that she never dared to try that again. Otherwise, she had been really good. Really!

She had come to love the human. It was her human now. She knew that somewhere in its heart, the human also knew that she was its dog. Perhaps if she wished really hard, she'd never have to leave.

So, she wished with all her heart. She wished on every little star she could see from the tiny balcony of their home that they would never part ways.

Because wishes did come true. This was a fact. She somehow just knew it!

All her wishes must have added up and paid off because the human started playing with her again. Then one day, it gave her a name.

"Pixie," it called her.

It had taken her into its arms. They had become a family!

That day, Pixie got a Mom who was of an entirely different species.

✦

Fluffers waited while both Pixie and Sia worked on strengthening their personal bond with the soul. His eyes caught sight of a shining, twinkling speck being pulled slowly closer to them.

"Whatever you girls are doing," he said, "it's working. I see your runaway soul. Keep at it!"

CHAPTER 7

MEETING SIA A.K.A. SI

She wriggled and cuddled up with her mother, her favourite sibling snoozing next to her. Right from the beginning of her life, she was a fierce and adventurous one. Always one to fight back if anything was even remotely a threat to the pack. Always ready for an adventure and to push the boundaries.

On a gloomy and overcast day, she and her favourite sibling ventured out.

"Do you wonder where Mother goes every day?" she had asked her brother.

"Yes."

"Wanna go see?" she turned around and asked him.

"Um…no!" her brother mumbled.

"Come on! It'll be fun!" she coaxed him into following her. They dashed out into the street, leaving their little safe-haven behind. She could see their mother trotting down the road far away. Her ears flopping and tail bobbing up and down as she walked.

"There she is!" she said, and they watched as their mother met with some of the other older dogs, who climbed out from under the 'vehicles' that stood on either side of the road. They were lucky that this was not a very busy area of town.

The two little furballs excitedly jumped across the nearly empty street and lost sight of their mother once they had crossed over. Now nervous, they tiptoed down the road in the direction they had seen their mother just moments before.

They reached a 'building' with a large gate in front of it. Both hesitating to go any further. They quickly realised why their mother had forbidden them from leaving the safety of their little home. Just stepping outside was so big that they immediately felt small and lost. They couldn't even fathom how large the rest of the world must be. Or how cruel.

Just like not every human was nice, not every dog had good intentions. Many of the dogs snapped and barked at them, as though they were trying to steal food from them! As soon as she and her brother had been spotted at the gate, they were shooed away by a couple of mean-looking humans with sticks. The two little ones cowered, their eyes shooting wide open with fear, and scrambled to hide under a vehicle standing close by.

An old, scruffy dog with a mean streak was already sitting under the vehicle. He let out a raspy laugh the moment he noticed the two tiny puppies.

"Lost little pups don't last long in this world," he said, with a mean growl.

"We are not lost!" she shot back, "we're just waiting for our mummy. She will be here any minute!" She was tiny, sure, but she would not let this nasty dog walk all over her.

"Why don't you two go *home* then? I'm sure your mummy will meet you there. She will get you some yummy food too!"

Her tummy growled at the mention of food. The rumble of her stomach was drowned by the snapping sound of thunder crackling through the sky. She huddled closer to her brother, who looked absolutely terrified.

"L-let's go home, please!" he begged.

"It's quite the storm!" The old dog laughed as the scared little pups huddled closer to each other.

"Get out of my space!" the mean dog snarled at them, satisfied as the startled pups cowered even more.

"I don't like sharing my shelter with lost little pups! Go home. If you can find it, that is," he added, as they scrambled out from under the vehicle, afraid of what the large old dog might do to them.

They were drenched within seconds, their fur sticking to their bodies. Desperate to catch the scent of their home or a glimpse of their mother, they sniffed around. But the rain had washed everything away. Now they were both truly directionless. The old dog was right they were indeed lost. They shuffled towards the wall behind them in search of some shelter, any shelter from the relentless rain beating down on them. But there was none. They took solace in the presence of each other, trying not to let fear get the better of them. Even so, they must have looked pitiful enough, for a kind-looking human walked up to them. They looked up at the human, amazed at the sheer height of the creature.

The human walked to the gates, sat down on a chair and produced a scrap of food, seemingly from thin air. It held the scrap out to them.

"Come on!" it said.

She moved ahead, but her brother held back,

"What if it *hurts* us?" he said.

"Don't be scared," she said, "I'm with you!"

Her brother followed her, and they both accepted the food from the human. Then the human picked the pair of them up and put them in a box by its feet, protecting them from the unyielding rain.

"See," she said, "now we're safe from the rain!"

They stayed there, and as evening passed and night fell, it turned cold. The kind human gave them a dirty rag that kept them warm, but the smell was horrible.

'It's better than dying, though,' she thought, and drifted off to sleep, only to wake up in the morning with a stabbing pain in her belly.

"You don't look so good," her brother said, watching as she threw up all her food from yesterday.

Yes, she did not feel very good. The pain in her stomach complained again. She had to poop. She got up, trying to find a place where she could do her business, her wobbly legs and blurry vision doing her no favours. Still, she managed a few steps and emptied her bowels, unable to hold it in anymore. The stink of whatever came out of her was revolting! No wonder her stomach had been hurting so badly.

She went back to her box, still looking and feeling terrible. The expression on her brother's face told her that she looked really, really sick.

"I'll go look for Mom," he said, clearly worried for her.

"No!" she protested. "I'm ok. Don't go, please." And she puked again.

"You are not ok!" he said tenderly as he walked away. "I'm going to look for Mom. I'll be back in a bit."

That was the last time she ever saw her favourite sibling.

As the day dragged on and evening turned to night, her heart sank. The pain in her stomach was constant as she waited for her brother to come back, hoping that, against all odds, he had found their mother and she would soon be with her family again. But no such thing came to pass, and she hid in her box, away from the mean world outside.

From the safety of her little shelter, she watched many humans and dogs walk in and out of the building. The kind human who had helped them in the rain gave her more scraps of food that she ate up and then regretted when her stomach hurt even more.

A sudden ruckus piqued her interest, and she took a little peek outside. Just then, a large dog charged at her. Shocked, she withdrew into her hiding place and stayed there for the rest of the night till morning dawned once more. And once more, there was no brother and no mother.

As she started to doze off, the mean old dog returned. “See, little pup, I told you that you won’t last long,” he taunted, seemingly satisfied at its own twisted wisdom.

“I’m still alive, though,” she weakly snapped back at him.

“Yes,” he narrowed his eyes. “I don’t see your brother anywhere. I wonder what happened to him! Hope the world’s not gobbled him up.”

“Shut up!” she snarled at the mean old dog.

“Oh, hush, little pup! Save all that energy. You don’t look so good. You will need it.”

She sat down and threw up again as the world spun around her.

A horrible thought crossed her mind: maybe the old grouch was right. ‘Maybe the world does swallow up little pups.’

'NO!' She could not think like that. She had to have hope.

It had been a couple of days since her brother had left her in search of their mother. She was feeling slightly better as the pain in her stomach dulled down some, though not completely gone; she could move around easily. Not feeling like a dying slug anymore, she made up her mind to go search for her mother and brother herself.

Just as she stepped out, her hope came in the form of a human she had seen go in and out of the building, accompanied by a grown-up brown dog with a black snout and floppy black ears. Both the human and the dog had a certain kindness about them. It appeared to her that the human had not seen her thus far, because the moment its eyes fell on her, the human squealed with pure joy! Her heart swelled at the sound.

The human hurried inside the building and came back with a bowl of yummy milk. She lapped all the milk up and finally felt full. But the tummy pain returned.

Seeing that she didn't look so good, the human picked her up and checked her all over. She had no idea how the human knew that she had tummy pains, but it did.

"Does your tummy hurt?" the human asked. "Do you want to come home?"

'YES!' Her heart screamed. 'Yes, I want to go home. I miss my mummy and all my brothers and sisters.'

The human carried her into the building and into a strange metal box that made a weird whirring noise as it moved. She could tell it was moving, and she could also tell that it was moving upwards.

The box stopped with a shudder, and its doors opened. The human still held her in its arms as it opened a door and stepped inside. This was the human's home.

But she wanted to go to *her* home!

"It's ok! Don't worry! You will be safe here," said a calm voice. The human set her down on the cool floor and walked away. That's when she noticed the other dog. It was the same dog, the one that she had seen go in and out of the building with the human. The one with the black snout and floppy ears. The calm voice belonged to this dog.

"Hi, little one, I'm Pixie."

"Pixie?"

"Yes," the older dog said. "It's the name that Mom gave me when she brought me home to live with her."

"Pixie, I'm scared," she whimpered. A little shiver shook her tiny body.

Pixie's eyes softened.

"Don't worry. Mom is really nice. A little crazy sometimes. But who isn't?"

"I just wanted to go to *my* home," Sia sniffled, "but this human brought me here to *its* home," she complained, tears forming in her eyes. "I'm never going to be able to go home. I'm never going to be able to see my family! Or my favourite brother!" she choked.

Pixie sat close to her, "Hey, little one, you *are* home. You *are* with family. We will walk with you every step of the way! So, wipe those tears away."

The human came back with a bundle of clean rags and a large bag. It then proceeded to bundle her up in the cloth and place her in the giant bag. This brought back memories for Pixie, and she smiled.

"We will go see a doctor, ok," the human said, looking straight at her.

She shot a worried look at Pixie, who had an amused expression on her face.

She noticed the smile on Pixie's face and grumbled at her, "Why are you smiling!"

When the human went back inside, Pixie said, "There is a human called 'doctor.' It will help you. Mom is taking you to this doctor because you look like you are sick. No need to worry so much."

"I'm allowed to be suspicious. The mean dog outside told us the world gobbles pups up! And I think it did gobble up my brother," she sniffling as she climbed out of the giant bag.

"That mean dog is just that - Mean. and nothing else. Don't listen to him. He has a very twisted way of looking at the World. He was just trying to scare you. The world is a nice place. You can take my word for it." Pixie smiled.

“Hey!” The human was back. “Get back in that bag!” it said and wagged its finger at her. It picked her up and put her back in the bag once again and closed it, leaving a little gap so she could poke her little head out.

And they were off!

Pixie gave her a reassuring nod when she looked back at her with worry on her face.

With her heart pounding in her chest, she wondered what she had gotten herself into this time.

‘Why could I not have just stayed at home? Why did I have to follow Mom? If anything, bad has happened to my brother, it is entirely my fault!’ She berated herself,

They travelled in a small vehicle. Everything outside moved fast, and it made her dizzy. For a moment, she thought she saw her mother with her brother and two other siblings on the side of the road. She smiled, feeling a bit relieved. They reached the doctor, who looked her over and said she had stomach trouble, then poked her with a needle. That hurt! But oddly, she was already feeling better.

Soon, they were back at the human's home. She ran to Pixie as soon as the human let her out of the bag.

As days passed, she was happy. She felt safe. Content that she did not have to sleep hungry. Every day, she woke up with hope in her heart, looking forward to spending time with Pixie and the human.

So, when suddenly, the human started pushing away from her and ignoring her when she brought it a toy she wanted to play with, it broke her heart.

"Did I do something wrong?" she asked Pixie. Tears were swimming in her eyes.

"No, you didn't. Mom is wondering if she should keep you here or not. But don't worry, she will give you a name soon."

"What do you mean, keep me? I never asked it to get me here, and I am not garbage that it can just throw away. What kind of a bad game is this human playing?"

"It's not a game. Some humans don't like creatures like us. They trouble the humans that take us in, so Mom really has to think before she decides to keep you or any other creature. It was the same for me. But then I wished on stars, and all of my wishes came true. Now, I live here with Mom."

"I want to wish on stars too. I want to stay here with you, Pixie."

"Let's do that then. Today, when the stars come out, let's both make wishes on as many stars as possible."

"Does that sort of thing really work, though?" Sia sounded sceptical.

"Mine did, I believe that if we believe with all of our heart, wishes come true."

That night, they sat on the balcony and made wishes on as many twinkling stars as they could.

A few days later, the human held her close and cried as she said, “I’m sorry. I was really bad to you for some days! I’m sorry. Never again!”

She put her down. “We’ll call you Sia,” she said as she wiped away tears that had trailed down her face. “What do you think, Pixie? Is Sia a good name?”

“Hi, Sia! What a pretty name!” Pixie said, tilting her head at her baby sister. “See. Our wishes came true.”

“Yes!” Sia was over the moon and jumped around the house all day. So much that it even annoyed Pixie a little.

“I can call it Mom too, now?” Sia asked.

“You could have called her Mom even before, Si.”

"Si." She thought about it for a bit, then said, "I like that pet name."

✦

Pixie and Sia opened their eyes. Saw what Fluffers was referring to. The soul was back. They could see it and feel its tug again. And now, they could even see the faint shimmer of the thin cord that attached them to the soul, even though the soul was still quite far away. Just being able to see it again had put their minds at ease.

"You girls did an amazing job!" Fluffers was all praises for both of them.

Something on Sia's head caught his attention. He squinted his eyes to look at what it was.

"What *is* that?" he tilted his head, this way then that.

Pixie could see it too, a shard-like thing dancing on Sia's head. It was tiny, but it was definitely there.

Sia shrank under the scrutiny of her companions.

Before they could make sense of what they were looking at, the soul shot past them and yanked on Pixie and Sia hard. They lost their balance and tried to reel the soul in.

CHAPTER 8

If There Are Gods, There Are Demons

The soul yanked hard on them. It reminded them of their morning walks. But here, the roles were reversed. They were on the receiving end of the pulling and tugging, the ones doing the wrangling. They had to admit, it was tough trying to control something that was so impulsive in its movements, and promised themselves they'd be better when Mom took them t on a walk. In fact, when anyone took them on a walk.

The soul pulled them one way, then the other. Fluffers followed, trying his best to keep up with the abrupt changes in direction.

The soul seemed to have no direction, but in truth, it was being pulled by something. And in turn, it was pulling Pixie and Sia thanks to their cord connection.

Fluffers had great instincts and latched himself on to Pixie's energy through their already established friendship once he understood what was going on.

The soul dragged them hither and thither for a while before a large gaping rip appeared in the space in front of them. Like a giant fish of the sea, the rift had swallowed them whole. They passed right into it before they could even react. They found themselves standing in a space that mirrored the fractal broken glass chamber of the Shadow god. Only this place was brighter, more inviting.

"Lost souls?" a voice rang in their heads. Its song-like hum lingered in their minds. They found themselves swaying to the sound of the voice. Pixie and Fluffers shook it off.

"Ooh, I feel all woozy," Sia slurred.

"Snap out of it, Si!" said Pixie.

"I want to, but it's so comforting."

"There is no use trying so hard, lost little souls," said the voice.

"I take what I want! And I have a lot of uses for lost souls," it said in a sing-song manner. The three were absolutely confused, unable to ascertain where the voice was coming from.

"Looking for me?" the voice said as an entity unfolded its presence from a singular point in front of them, its translucent black body undulating like it was made of thin, wispy smoke.

The last to appear was its head, bright like the sun, a swirling vortex so bright that Pixie, Sia and Fluffers had to shield their eyes from it. All around this entity, wispy tendrils trailed as it moved, shooting out and catching wayward souls that floated too close to it, shoving them at its glowing head, where they endlessly circled, around the bright sun-like centre, practically captivated by the glow.

Mom's soul was completely enchanted by the entity, and was willingly trying to move towards it, dragging Pixie, Sia and Fluffers along.

"Si, keep a strong hold on Mom," Pixie warned as Sia started to slowly get pulled in.

"It's been an eternity since I've had the pleasure of consuming fully awake souls!" Its honey voice dripped with excitement. "You're all going to be my most delicious meal. Oh boy! What a treat!"

✦

They felt anxious in the presence of this demonic monster, which exuded the most alluring and comforting light to attract its prey. Behind the sense of false comfort was a demon waiting to consume them and lick its fingers after.

Fear bubbled up from somewhere deep inside them. Slick like hot tar.

Together, Pixie, Sia and Fluffers tried to pull the soul closer to themselves. But, even if they managed to catch the soul, *where could they go?*

They had no idea how they had entered the place. Getting out was an even bigger mystery.

The soul swayed closer and closer to the light. A black smoky tendril whipped out and caught it, reeling it in towards the swirling vortex. Pixie, Sia and Fluffers were violently dragged in, right behind the soul. They spun faster and faster.

As they got closer to the centre, they noticed that it was made of many colourful lights, packed so closely that from a distance it just looked like one giant blob of white. Each spot of colour was a place, they realised. Many different scenes whipped past them as they gained momentum, feeling like water going down a drain.

They were abruptly thrown into one of the spots of colour and came to a rolling stop on the soft, undulating grass beneath them.

They scrambled up and looked around. A cool breeze brushed past them, and there was soft sunlight playing on their fur. It was like they were back on Earth.

"The illusion is flawless!" Fluffers said, his brow knitted in contemplation.

"Illusion?" Sia asked, her eyes still full of amazement.

"This is not really Earth, Si," he said. "Look at the sky, look at the grass."

Pixie and Sia looked. Really looked. The sky looked normal one moment and flickered the next, turning into glass-like shards. The grass did the same.

"What's happening!"

"It's a prison," Fluffers stated, in a very matter – of - fact way.

"Prison?" Pixie and Sia said, alarmed.

"It's a beautiful prison! It's how this demon traps the souls, is my theory. It creates a beautiful and comforting place for souls. Something that will put their minds at ease." Fluffers started pacing while he thought. "I'm pretty sure that each soul it has caught will have a prison of its own, something unique to each soul. It's this demon's way of keeping its hold on the soul."

"I couldn't have said it better myself." A deep, glassy voice chipped in, making Sia jump ten feet up.

CHAPTER 9

SHOWDOWN

A tinkling sound materialized behind them and the three whipped around. There stood the Shadow god.

"H-how ar-e y-you?" Fluffers stammered, seemingly lost for words.

"Fluffers. I thought you were more articulate. Moments ago, you analysed the situation perfectly!"

"I'm sorry, I was just taken by surprise."

"Don't bully my friend!" Sia fired back at the god. Fluffers being addressed as a friend by Sia brought a little smile to both Pixie's and Fluffer's faces; Both exchanging amused glances.

"Anyone would be surprised if you skulked around and snuck up on them," Sia berated.

"Little one! I'm not skulking!" The god was completely taken aback at being addressed as though he were some common thug in his own home.

"This is my domain. I can very well go where I please," The god stated with an air of pride. "Plus, you should know, I'm not skulking; *you* are the one who brought me here, little one." He gave Sia one of his shifting smiles.

Sia looked utterly surprised, and so were Pixie and Fluffers. "No, I didn't! Why would I get you along?"

Then she remembered the strange feeling when the Shadow god had placed a quick pat on her head. Understanding dawned on her face.

"Ah…Now you understand!" said the god.

"That thing on Si's head, was you?" Fluffers asked the god.

"Yes, my dear boy. It was a small part of my existence that I left there so I could keep a close eye on you all."

The Shadow god's jittering smile was beginning to annoy Sia down to her bones. "You," she said, "Are you a creepy stalker too? Along with being a skulker?" she said, her voice dramatically loud.

Pixie was horrified, "Si!"

"If it's your domain, why did you have to do that to sneakily tag along with us? You could have just came along. Not like we could have said 'no,' even if we wanted to."

"But I couldn't, little one. This demon, eating all the souls, is a tricky one. It has hidden itself well from me. Always slipping from my grasp. If I just came along with you, it would have never shown itself. I had to make myself as inconsequential as possible."

The Shadow continued, "Lucky for me, you three came along. I knew that it would not be able to resist the chance to eat awake souls, and it was my only way to draw the demon out."

“You used us as bait?!” Sia was aghast. “Why do all gods think they can do whatever they want!”

Pixie scrambled towards Sia. “Shhhh. Siiii!”

“She-she didn’t mean that,” Pixie said, trying her best to do some damage control. Her head low, and eyes looking up at the Shadow god, she could have won an award for the guilty face she had just pulled on.

The tension dispersed somewhat. The god smiled, “You are right, little one. I needed your help. Demons are tricky. I must admit, I might have never found it if it were not for the three of you. You have my thanks.”

“Also, yes, I did use you as bait, and I'm not proud of it.”

The Shadow looked directly at Sia, “I’m sorry. Look at it this way, little one. You three are true heroes; you have saved not only your Mom’s soul, but all of these other lost souls.”

Something akin to a heartbeat ran through the space as the Shadow god spoke, "The demon knows that I'm here," the god cautioned.

"Now, it's time for you to leave this place. It will soon get ugly, and you don't want to get caught up in any of that. As agreed, you may take your soul. But remember, it can only leave my domain if it recognises you. It's the only way," the shadow god said as it stepped out of their way.

Pixie and Sia turned to the soul and saw that it had now taken the form of their Mom. She looked happy and content as she stared at a giant crystal tree in the distance. The tree was immense, standing tall and merging into the shimmering sky. It truly was a scene to behold! Glittering lights bounced off their faces as they made their way to their Mom, with Pixie leading the way and Sia following her close behind.

"When she recognises you, don't turn and look back, no matter what," whispered Fluffers, them as they passed by.

Pixie and Sia tentatively approached their Mom, where she stood transfixed, captivated by the shimmer of the giant tree.

The closer they got, the more anxious they felt. Afraid that one wrong step would spook her and send her soul flying away. Another rumble passed below their feet. This one was stronger. They froze. Fear gripped their hearts as they looked for any reaction from their Mom. Nothing.

She stood in the same spot, wind drifting past her, brushing her short hair over her serene face.

With a relieved sigh, they moved on. When they were close enough, Pixie stepped ahead and booped Mom's hand with her nose. Mom's focus instantly shifted, and she looked down to see Pixie and the purest smile, full of joy, took over Mom's face, as though she had never expected to see them here. There was recognition in her eyes. Tears rolled down her face as she called out,

"Pixie! Sia!".

The moment Pixie knew that Mom had recognised them, she turned around and ran. Sia followed. The soul cord between them and Mom glowed bright — a sure sign that Mom's soul would follow them.

Fluffers joined them.

"Good! The soul remembers you," they heard the Shadow god say.

"Now, little ones," the god said, as another destructive shudder passed below their feet, "Let's get you home."

With that, the Shadow god flicked a finger and opened a small portal a few paces in front of them.

"Hurry along and go home!"

The three ran towards the portal the god had created, the soul following close behind. Just as they were reaching the portal, jagged shards came hurling in at them, but still they ran. They had to get to that portal; they had to get Mom back! At any cost!

The soul had caught up to them now. It was back in its glowing orb form. It kept up and stayed between Pixie and Sia, who moved closer to it, in an attempt to shield it from harm. More shards rained down, slicing lines of fire on them. They were so close now. A large shard came hurling and planted itself in front of the portal, blocking their way out. They came to a frantic stop, coming face to face with their own reflections in the glossy surface. More shards whizzed past them, and they ducked, tucking their heads under their paws, bracing for the glassy fragments to rip right through them. But when no such thing happened, they cautiously looked up to see that the shards were floating inches above them, stopped by an unseen shield the god had created.

The god was standing with his palm open, as though holding the glassy shards motionless in their trajectory. He curled his fingers close, and the shards crumbled into a haze of shimmering mist that glittered around them.

The demon roared! Its previously sweet sing-song voice had changed into a harsh chittering sound that better fit its horrible character.

"T-t-these ar-r-r-re m-m-m-my-y-y s-s-s-souls-s-s-s," it let out a hissy scream, as all the souls swirling around its bright head scrambled and scattered. It shot out its many wispy tentacles and caught as many souls as it could, shoving them back towards its head. But many of the souls had already reached the Shadow god and taken refuge behind him. The Shadow conjured up a fragmented wall to shield the souls.

Enraged, the demon shot its tentacles at the wall to grab the souls behind it. But the moment its tentacle made contact with the wall, it burst into a puff of smoke, making the demon bellow out in agony. The wall remained undamaged.

"Serves you right!" Fluffers shouted out at the demon, bringing its attention to them.

An army of wispy tentacles darted at them. As they dodged left and right, Pixie quickly tucked the soul under one of her floppy ears.

"Sorry," Fluffers knew he had messed up.

"If we die, I'm going to haunt you forever!" Sia threatened the old dog again.

The Shadow god folded into himself, disappearing.

"Did he just run away?!" Sia was astonished at the audacity of this god!

A smoky tentacle shot past Pixie's face as she dodged another.

The demon was trying to swarm her.

"Fluff!" Sia called out to Fluffers. "It's going after Mom's soul!" She said as she watched Pixie dodge as many of the tentacles as she could. Some made contact and left a burning welt on her.

Pixie was engulfed in a smoky mass of tentacles. Sia and Fluffers ran to her aid and dragged her out of the tangled chaos. She looked terrified and defeated.

"It took Mom!" Pixie broke down in tears.

"Pix, I see it," Sia had her eyes locked on one tentacle that held the bright light of Mom's soul "Come on!" The little orb was pulsating as though calling for help.

Pixie's eyes widened as she saw it. Sia was already off, chasing after it.

Pixie and Fluffers ran after her.

From the corner of his eye, Fluffers caught the Shadow god materialise behind the demon, which had its complete focus on its prey in front of it.

The three of them ran at top speed, reaching the demon's head just as the tentacle let go of Mom's soul, shoving it into the stampede of other souls it had managed to recapture. The cord connection they had managed to re-form was once again threatening to fade away, but they tracked the soul down, hanging on to the flimsy connection that remained.

"Si! She is this way," Pixie called out as she abruptly changed direction.

Mom's soul was motionless, eerily calm as many souls around her dashed away, creating a storm of panicked chaos. It was as though it knew that they would come and get it.

Pixie, Sia and Fluffers ran to Mom's soul. The orb was growing brighter in an understanding that they were near it. Pixie quickly tucked the soul under her ear once more.

Just when they turned around to move out of the chaos. A sharp, fragmented spear-like object shot out exactly where Mom's soul had been moments ago.

They cowered down again as the Demon let out a bloodcurdling cry, and a tremble of a shockwave rippled past them.

Once the embers of the Demon's scream fizzled away, they peeked from under the safety of their paws. The god was standing behind the Demon, his form was as large as the Demon's, larger even. The god was furious. His face reflected the anger in his heart. One of his fragmented, glassy hands was plunged right through the Demon's glowing head.

Waves of electric energy rippled out from where the god had stabbed the Demon, then an explosive burst rushed past them as the Demon's head burst with a resounding explosion, and they all tumbled backward unable to hold their ground in the face of the destructive shockwave.

All the chaos abruptly died away, and there was silence save for the tinkling of the Shadow god as he walked towards the trio. No demon in sight.

"That took quite a bit out of me!" the god said. "I'm sorry you got trapped between all that."

"Wouldn't have happened if you had opened the portal closer to us!" Sia said, still locked in her relentless feud.

"Yes, little one. You once again have my deepest apologies. For that and for using you all as bait."

The Shadow god once again opened the portal, "You are free to go, with my deepest thanks." He said as he gave them a slight bow in gratitude.

✦

Just as they reached the portal, he spoke again, "Hold on, little ones. You seem to have something that belongs to me."

Fluffers and Pixie turned around, confused.

"Feisty little one," the Shadow god addressed Sia, who turned around, guilt written all over her face.

"Release them," the Shadow god commanded.

In the chaos, Sia had let a whole lot of souls attach to her, hoping that no one would notice. She shook her body, and a swarm of souls popped out of her, their cords attached to her.

The Shadow god rubbed his hand down his face, clearly exhausted with the events of the day "No sneaking souls out, little one!" He sighed.

"They just attached themselves to me," said Sia petulantly.

"Oh, did they?"

"Come here," the Shadow god motioned her close, and she was pulled towards him, her collection of souls trailing along behind her. Once she reached him, the Shadow god got to work, cutting the connections the souls had formed with Sia. Her face fell with each severed connection, and tears filled her eyes.

"No need to be so sad, little one." The Shadow god comforted her.

"Their fate is so cruel!" Sia sounded truly overcome by sadness.

"They have finished serving a purpose they had agreed to. They were aware of this fate. We are all serving some purpose, little one, including us gods." The Shadow god comforted her in his own way.

Once all the connections were severed, the Shadow god placed another pat on her head, removing the undulating shard he had placed there. "You are all done!"

"Aren't you going to punish me for trying to take the souls?"

"If I punish you after you helped me find and destroy that demon, I'd have to call myself a demon now, wouldn't I. You are free to go," the god smiled, and Sia ran to Pixie and Fluffers, who were waiting for her at the portal.

Sia noticed that Mom's soul was back in its human form. She ran to them with a pep in her step.

CHAPTER 10

HOME IS WHERE THE EARTH IS

They were on Earth. The air felt familiar, but they weren't home. This was a strange place. Clean to a fault. There were many beds that held humans who did not look very healthy. Other humans moved about the room. Taking care of the unhealthy-looking humans.

In one of these beds, Pixie and Sia noticed, was their Mom's physical body, but she looked different. There were a whole lot of tubes and wires attached to her. Her eyes were sunken, her skin pale, and all her hair was gone. The sight broke their hearts.

"What happened to you, Mom?" Sia softly asked Mom's soul, looking up at her.

Mom's soul knelt beside her and stroked her head, "Nothing, Si, I just had a little accident."

Pixie placed her head on Mom's knee so she could get head pats, too. Mom petted Pixie with her other hand, then hugged them tight. "Both of you brought me back! No. The three of you brought me back," Mom's soul said as she pulled Fluffers in for a hug, too. "I promise I will be fine in no time!"

She let go of them and watched as her little girls walked around her and stood by the bed that held her physical form.

Mom's soul understood what they wanted her to do. "Thank you for coming to get me, all three of you! I really was lost," she smiled.

She placed a kiss on their heads and merged back with her body. There was another loud snap as Mom's soul string attached to her physical form again.

Mom instantly stirred, setting off several alarms. People in blue clothes and white coats rushed in and fussed over her body. Some were tending to their mom, and others were tending to the machines that were erratically beeping. "Well, that's that," Fluffers said. The three of them waited and watched the scene play out.

Mom let out a tired groan and opened her eyes to little slits, looking right at the spot where the three of them were.

“She is back,” Sia said, a stream of tears falling from her eyes.

“Yes, she is.” Pixie sniffled. “We should get back too.”

“Fluff, thank you for helping us so much!” Sia gave the old dog her most genuine smile.

“That’s what friends are for, Si,” he said.

“I will try not to snap at you when we meet on our walks,” said Sia.

“That’s very kind! Thank you!”

With that, the three made their way back to their own bodies.

When Pixie and Sia entered their own bodies, they ran to grandma, grandpa and their aunts, jumping, their tails wagging with uncontained excitement.

"What's up with the two of you?" Their aunts said and smiled at them.

EPILOGUE

EPILOGUE

The god watched as the human soul berated Sia once she reached the three of them waiting for her at the portal. He smiled fondly at the bond these souls shared with each other. Then they all stepped through the portal and left their domain.

✦

Pixie and Sia were content after their adventure. They had saved Mom's soul! They would see her again! No matter how long it took for Mom to get home, they would wait for her and stick by her side till she was completely healthy.

For now, they would be on their best behaviour.

✦

"Hey! Si!" It was Fluffers.

Sia ran to him, dragging the dogwalker behind her. She snuggled up to the old dog, "Hi," she said as she smiled at him.

"This is new," the walker said, undoubtedly surprised at Sia's changed demeanour towards the old German Shepherd.

Pixie smiled and walked past the walker. "Hey, Fluffers!" she said.

"Hey to you both! I just wanted to ask, next time I need any help, will I be welcome to ask the two of you?"

"Of course!" they said.

"We are all, like, best friends now, old man!" Sia said, her tail wagging at lightspeed.

AUTHOR'S NOTE

In October 2024, I suffered a sudden stroke. While I was in the ICU, I had a vivid dream where I was standing in a lush green field. My focus was captivated by something I can't quite remember. Suddenly, I felt something nudge my hand. I looked down, and to my utter surprise, there were my baby girls, Pixie and Sia. I remember thinking, 'What are you doing here?'

The moment I looked at them, they turned around and ran. I called out to them, but they did not stop. I ran after them, and the next thing I remember is waking up in an ICU bed, a whole plethora of machines beeping around me. People gave me uncertain looks as I called out for my little girls to wait for me to catch up to them.

This might have been a dream. But I like to think of it as a memory. The whole thing felt so real, and the feel of Pixie's wet nose as she nudged my hand is something I will never forget.

I believe my girls brought me back from some place that beings rarely return from, and I am ever grateful!

AS A SIDE NOTE:

I would like to implore people to adopt street animals. We need love; they have plenty of it. They need a home, and we can provide it. It's a win-win situation.

Together, we can put an end to puppy mills and the atrocities of the breeding industry.

Let's give homes to the ones in need of them instead of creating more little creatures that sometimes end up living the worst possible life because they are the weakest in the litter.

Not to mention the animals that are subjected to repeated forced breeding without regard for their health or well-being to create said puppies and kittens to fulfil the demands of this devilish industry that has no soul.

No one talks of 'Humanity' when innocent creatures are just discarded once our human greed is satisfied.

If we believe that the care of this planet has been placed in our hands, let's be more responsible!

ACKNOWLEDGEMENT

I would like to thank my family and friends who stood by me throughout my recovery and then while I was writing this book.

A special thank you to both my sisters for giving me critical feedback at each stage of the development of 'The Worldwalkers.' I'm sure I've annoyed them extensively.

Without all my pets until today, and all of the animals I have crossed paths with, I'd never be the person I am today. So, an eternal thanks to them all.

And lastly, a heartfelt sorry to Carrom, my sister's cat, whom I have relentlessly troubled all through 2025. I'm sure she would maul me in my sleep if she could.